Hide and Seek

Written and illustrated

by

Judith King

Let's all play hide and seek!

Grandma Rabbit closed her eyes

and did not peek.

One, two, three, four...

Willow made a plan

and off she ran.

"She won't find me!"

She hid herself behind a tree.

Aspen made a plan

and off she ran.

"I'll make her laugh!"

She hid herself inside the bath.

Alder made a plan

and off he ran.

"I know!" he said.

He hid himself beside the shed.

Rowan made a plan
and off he ran.

"She won't see me!

This plant pot is the place to be!"

Hazel made a plan

and off she ran.

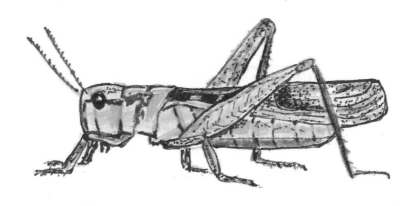

"She'll have to search for hours
and hours,
If I crouch down amongst these
flowers!"

All were quiet, not a sound.

Waiting their turn to be found.

But from Grandma there was not a peep,

for she had fallen fast asleep!

Printed in Great Britain
by Amazon